THE MAN IN THE STREET

THE MAN
IN THE STREET

Ann Chwatsky

E. P. DUTTON

NEW YORK

In memory of my mother,
Gladys Schneider Coleman,
who first taught me
to look at men.

Copyright © 1989 by Ann Chwatsky ▲ All rights reserved. Printed in the U.S.A. ▲ No part of this publication may be reproduced or transmitted in any form or by any means, electronic or mechanical, including photocopy, recording, or any information storage and retrieval system now known or to be invented, without permission in writing from the publisher, except by a reviewer who wishes to quote brief passages in connection with a review written for inclusion in a magazine, newspaper, or broadcast. ▲ Published in the United States by E. P. Dutton, a division of NAL Penguin Inc., 2 Park Avenue, New York, N.Y. 10016. ▲ Published simultaneously in Canada by Fitzhenry and Whiteside, Limited, Toronto. ▲ Library of Congress Cataloging-in-Publication Data ▲ Chwatsky, Ann. ▲ The man in the street/Ann Chwatsky. — 1st ed. ▲ p. cm. ▲ ISBN 0-525-24714-9 ▲ 1. Labor and laboring classes—United States—Interviews. ▲ I. Title. ▲ HD8072.5.C48 1989 ▲ 331'.0973—dc19 88-11105 CIP ▲ Designed by Nancy Etheredge ▲ Printed in Spain ▲ 10 9 8 7 6 5 4 3 2 1 ▲ First Edition ▲ Printed by Printer Industria Gráfica, S.A. Barcelona, Spain. D.L.B. 46768-88

If you will let me, I will wish you in your future what all men desire—enough work to do, and strength enough to do your work.

—RUDYARD KIPLING, address to medical students, 1908

He builded better than he knew,
The conscious stone to beauty grew.

—RALPH WALDO EMERSON, "The Problem"

ACKNOWLEDGMENTS

For Marc, Julie, and Howard, who were always there every step of the way. For Peter, who got it all started, and for Meg, whose enthusiasm, unflagging support, and wisdom got the book done. And for Nancy, who cared about it and designed it with feeling. For Anoush and Vincent and Annahid and Diana Labs: I could not have done it without you. And for Zina, for help in putting it together. And for my assorted scouts across the country—thanks to you all.

And to all *The Men in the Streets*—thanks for your time, your openness, and your cooperation. I hope I did you justice—you were all great.

In preparing for this book I read with much interest some books that deal with the working class man. Most memorable to me were *Working* by Studs Terkel, and *Worlds of Pain: Life in the Working Class Family* by Lillian Breslow Rubin.

FOREWORD

As a photographer I have always been fascinated by looking at other peoples' lives. While photographing these men I became aware of another dimension to this voyeurism—that of a woman's appreciation for a man's body, of the opportunity to watch and observe and evaluate all while hidden by the camera. It was as if I was entering a man's world, but with my own perspective. Perhaps it was my way of emulating the behavior of the men in the streets who comment and whistle at the women walking by.

My work is the product of a collaborative venture. The men I photographed demonstrated a willingness to be open, to share, and to be captured in words and on film. Their initial reaction was one of pure macho, but often the facade was lowered to reveal tenderness, boyishness, prettiness, brashness, strength, sexiness, and intelligence. Intrigued by the idea of the book, there was much that they wanted to communicate. They took pride in being part of an effort to tell people who they were and what they thought about. I hope I have done these men justice.

Throughout the ages, writers, philosophers, and artists have endeavored to capture the true spirit of the workingman. Our popular culture has contributed other images of workers. But what are these men really like—these men who build the bridges we cross, construct the houses we live in, the buildings we work in, and the roads we walk and drive on? My aim was to create an awareness of people we see every day yet seldom notice.

Some days I would go to a previously chosen site where the men would be expecting me. Other days, it was serendipity. I would randomly choose a location—perhaps a town where I knew there was an active construction site or, in a major city, I would explore a twenty-block radius. I was drawn to particular sites for different reasons: the lighting, the composition of a building, the interaction among several men, or more usually, the look of a certain worker. Often, it was the lines of his body as he was working, or the look in his eyes that drew me to that location.

Only once or twice was I not welcome when I photographed. The usual response to my camera and inquiries was positive and enthusiastic. Easily engaged in conversation, these men enjoyed bantering and joking, yet were able to take themselves seriously as well. I met men of profound intelligence, who were able to articulate a keen awareness of themselves and their work, and men who were quiet and "just doing their job."

I often felt a kinship with the artists of the past, particularly of the Renaissance, who went into the streets to sketch the natural beauty of the "everyday" man. At times, the classic, idealized works of the Greek and Roman sculptors would come to mind as I observed these men unconsciously assuming poses.

There were similarities and differences in the workingmen I encountered as I crossed the country. In some areas the workers had a real sense of continuity and security. Along with this sometimes came a feeling of their being stuck in one place, at a dead end. In other parts of the country, I found men cherishing their uniqueness. As one worker put it, "We have the rugged individualism of the cowboy ethic to live up to." It is as if they are involved in creating their own new America.

Teamwork and trust are crucial to safety in construction work. Handing over heavy or dangerous materials, supporting the ladder for another, doing the preliminaries for a job the next worker has to build on are all closely linked physical tasks in which these men must rely on each other. In addition to this forced dependence, I was also struck by a spirit of camaraderie—a sense of fun akin to the joy of little boys who share a secret pact. Men in the street often take personal physical risks in their work. At any time, a false move could cause severe bodily damage or loss of life. Living with this danger seems to foster a rugged independence and strength that I grew to respect. But it also helps foster interdependence, a sense of community from taking risks together, a rite of passage into the fraternity. This entry is furthered by the need for teamwork.

My fascination with the subject of the workingman has very early roots. I grew up in a family of builders. As a child I remember visiting my father at work and being given a hammer and nails and a wooden board with which to amuse myself. I would spend hours awkwardly but deliberately hammering away, dreaming about building big structures like my father did.

Many people today feel that they spend their days performing tasks that have no purpose or meaning—going to endless meetings, shuffling papers, making plans, and then revising strategies. These men don't. Without meaning to simplify or to over-idealize physical labor, there is pleasure in engaging in a task that results in a tangible product that is satisfying in a deep-rooted way. Starting a task and visualizing some final physical product is part of the appeal of the process of photography for me. When it all works—it is wonderful. To the men out there on the street that I met, thank you for making it wonderful.

INTRODUCTION

When I was growing up in New York in the 1940s and '50s I took the subways everywhere. And in late afternoon and early evening the subway cars bound for Brooklyn were permeated by a distinctive odor: sharp and pungent and oddly sweet. It was the smell of drying sweat—which is to say, the odor of manual labor.

That honest and very human odor is one of the many things that have vanished from New York. Most of our factories have closed; the lighting fixture plant that once employed my father is now a condominium, filled with young professionals. The few men who still work with their backs and their hands now drive home after work, to the dubious pleasures of the suburbs. The children of those dirty, sweat-coated men of my youth work with computers in clean well-lighted places. They are teachers or lawyers or doctors. Many have moved West or to Florida where there are no subways and the hard canyons of New York are a bleak, distant memory. Their educations were purchased through the back-breaking toil of their fathers—men of a generation shaped by depression and war. Few generations of American men have been so radically different from their fathers' generations. The children of the men I saw and smelled in the subways now labor without fear of physical danger on their jobs. Their hands are smoother. Their bodies are softer. They do not, alas, seem more happy.

But, as the photographs in this book demonstrate so splendidly, manual labor continues to be a fact of American life. Men (and increasing numbers of women) use the energy of their bodies to place things in the world that did not exist before: houses, buildings, bridges, roads. They place brick upon brick. They bend cables. They tear out rotted or decayed parts of old structures and replace them with newer parts, thus salvaging what is useful from the past. They walk the high iron of skyscrapers. They enter the dark tunnels of sewer systems, power plants, telephone tunnels. The pay is much better now, but the dangers remain the same. In most manual labor there is always a risk of death. One wrong step, one missed signal and you could be gone.

In almost all cases these tough, brave men are members of a team, working in unison with others; no single person, after all, can erect a skyscraper or a bridge. And that shared labor (combined with physical danger) creates a sense of fraternity that is simply not the same as the social connections that are built among white-collar workers. In some ways, men who have built bridges together are like men who have fought wars together. They know the common dangers they have faced and what they have done to overcome them and how each of them survived; often, they remain alive to work another day *because* of each other.

In many respects, the present generation of blue-collar workers is the best educated in U.S. history. Manual labor is no longer the badly paid refuge of the illiterate, or of men who can do nothing else. Many have attended school to learn to read blueprints, make engineering calculations, and handle the array of increasingly complicated tools. In many of these photographs you see those tools: ranging from the traditional shovel and hammer to hi-los and earth movers. These tools are dumb instruments until they are used by men. There is a glorious elegance to men who know and love their tools; the tools become extensions of their bodies *and* their minds, as they are wielded in a special, almost private rhythm. Baseball players use their tools in this way: swinging bats, kneading gloves. And so do musicians. The man who loves his work is always like this with the instruments of his craft.

There is, of course, a macho swagger to many of these men. It displays itself in its worst form in those familiar sidewalk rituals at lunch hour. Women go by; the men make remarks, sounds, whistles, all charged with sexual innuendo. The women often walk straight ahead, eyes locked on the middle distance. A few hurl killer remarks. They almost always hear dirty laughter. Some feminists are infuriated by the crudity of the experience. But there is more to these men than that lunch hour cliché.

Their most important quality is pride. Most of these men are proud of their skills, their mastery of difficult tasks. They are proud, too, that they are working at these jobs, making good salaries, providing food and clothing and shelter to wives and children. And, they are proud of their bodies. Most of them don't go to gyms or health clubs; they don't discuss diets or cholesterol; they eat heavily and many of them drink hard. But while they are young they act as if they are immortal. They drive themselves hard and use their bodies as if they are tools that will never wear out. But, like athletes, they slowly learn that decay is inevitable. After thirty they grow fleshier. They move more slowly. Those who have mastered their skills have no fear of the future; they have gone through their apprenticeships and as journeymen they will always work. But they probably also have been hurt on the job at least once, and if they haven't they will be in the future. They have learned that the hard invincibility of youth never lasts. They become men of extraordinary skill, walking anthologies of lore, craft, mistakes, solutions—or they go off to softer work.

Something about all of this is tragic, in the sense that life itself is always a tragedy that ends in death. But, it helps to explain the macho swagger: most of it is a bluff. Such men want to tell strangers that they are the best ironworkers, hardest drinkers, toughest saloon fighters, and greatest lovers; and few of them believe this for a minute. They feel they are men of value because of what they must do every working day of their lives. But these are people who will never appear on the cover of *People* magazine. Not many novels are written about them, and their lives have been examined in only a few movies. They don't end up on posters in the rooms of college sophomores. But men like these have built America. So they are saying: Hey, look at me. I'm important too.

This book agrees with them. These men *are* important. At least as important as the dozens of cops and lawyers and doctors who inhabit the world presented by television. Without them the physical plant of this country would collapse; many abstract visions of the future could never be brought into existence. Looking at their faces we can only imagine their lives, their sorrows and small victories, the cutting edge of their humor. But I am reminded by their presence of the best job I ever had. The year was 1951, and I was an apprentice sheet-metal worker in the Brooklyn Navy Yard. I was sixteen. That year the nation's aircraft carriers were being converted to be used by jets, and the flight decks and decks below had to be ripped out, rebuilt, and strengthened. I was assigned to work with a black man named Harry at the task of removing the heavy metal bulkheads on the first deck. Harry used the acetylene torch, burning away the edges of the bulkheads, his face hidden behind a mask. When he was finished the wall remained in place, held up by tacks of unburned metal. And then I would walk up to these walls with a huge hammer . . . and smash them down. When they fell I walked upon them as if trampling the body of a slain opponent. The noise was ferocious and Harry always cheered. We'd drink some milk (it was said to coat the lungs against the fumes of the burning metal) and go on to the next bulkhead.

I worked many other jobs after that one. But my life took another turn. And the sense of physical power, the feeling of triumph over an implacable object, the surging belief that I could hold my own at the side of men—I never felt that way again.

PETE HAMILL
New York, August 1988

THE MAN IN THE STREET

I am in a different place every day—I'm not sitting behind a desk. I have been doing this for eight years. I put in gas pipes. There are leaks and it can sometimes be dangerous. I am more confident now in my gas ability. I can smell when something is wrong. Doing this for the rest of my life is something I may do. Some days are bad, though.

I've been doing bricklaying and cement mixing for thirty-five years. I'm getting tired; I am ready for retirement.

I've watched the city grow. Now they build better buildings because they use more steel, there is more structure. The most wonderful thing is the jokes with the guys—that's the whole thing.

We don't work with girls, so when we see them, we get excited. If you are in an office and you see girls all the time, you wouldn't be excited. It wouldn't be a big deal. But this way when you see a pretty girl, you have to talk to her. It used to be that we tipped our hats to the ladies. Now the ladies curse you out if you say anything. Buildings have gotten better but people have not—they are lousier.

On this job, we all watch out for each other. If you are not scared to work hard and you *do* work hard, you will be successful no matter what you do. You have to take pride in what you do. I wanted to start young so I can retire young.

This work makes you seem stupid and ignorant to others. If they see you in a deli, all dirty in the middle of work, they think of you as a two-dollar-an-hour laborer who digs holes. I probably make more than the ones there wearing the fancy suits.

The girls driving by is all part of the scene. They go around the block and they scream. You laugh and scream back. It's fun—it's all just part of it.

I like what I do. I like the guys, including the boss. The women do like to look at the men.

I would like to be a painting contractor someday—have to get all the licenses. Right now it's hard to find good housing for the wife and my child.

I've been working for Bob since 1973. We are a small company; we have good quality control. Everything is changing today. The bedrock of America—the families and small businesses—are beginning to disintegrate. We think everyone should be engaged in manual labor. The boss and the laborers should mingle. "Condescend to seek lower people," the Scriptures say that. That is why God dwelled among men. He was still God, though.

We are all Christians, the Lord is the mainstay. The Lord is the foundation, just like laying the blocks is the foundation. Life is like laying blocks; the Lord is the foundation.

The workingman is really everyone. The successful ones, they don't forget where they come from. Those that aren't successful, they forget.

I'm from Chicago, Illinois, originally. I'm glad I'm laying blocks in the sunshine [Arizona]. It is also economic necessity. What I do is in the classic tradition of masonry. But the business is changing—it's switching from stone to wood. My great-grandfather was from Hamburg, Germany, and he was a monument cutter; he worked with stone.

It has been scientifically documented that everyone needs physical activity. Many workers spend their time after work jogging and working out. We [this crew] don't have to do that. We spend time after work on intellectual pursuits—like church and social events. We don't mess around—no alcohol, sex, or drugs because we believe in the Lord.

I like the demolition work. We take things apart—we wreck anything. I used to be a cop until a year ago. I did that for thirteen years. Police work is a lot of political bullshit. The mental strain is less here, and it leaves me time for the wife and kids. I did both jobs for a while to see if I could make it. Now I'm just on my own and I'm doing great.

I used to live in California and Texas. I used to box and I went to Mohammed Ali's camp, but I wasn't a pro. I've been stabbed, beat up, and kicked as a cop. What I'm doing now is not safe—you have to be careful. When you are taking down whole buildings anything could fall. Everyone always said that I was good at destroying things anyway, so I might as well destroy buildings.

I keep in pretty good shape doing this; it will keep me healthy. The elements are a problem. You gotta take care of your body. Some other guys might say, I can't do that. I don't say no to anything. I'd like to be a millionaire and not work at all. We don't want unions out here. But the middle-class worker is just about out of the system.

I've jumped out of cars while they were still running, I've gotten arrested. I'm a gentleman now, I've calmed down. The demolition gets out the aggression. I've had a lot of fun in my life.

I can't be around men who do posturing and use racial and sexist slurs. A lot of what men say about how they like to work with their hands is just posturing. Workers have the old cowboy image. They want to carry it on more, so they do macho, self-perpetuating talk. I work with two or three men and we know each other well and we are not like that. If you are making a good living, it's hard to be negative.

My father left being a painter when it became a union job. My uncles and father were German housepainters. They were so neat they did not use drop cloths. So when I was ten or eleven my dad built houses and I used to help out. I'd clean up. It was a family project—I'd tag along. For me, building has always been good pickup work. I did a little bit of it in college. I went to school for business administration; I didn't know what I wanted. I was in the Vietnam War, then went back to college. I worked in a day-care center and liked that and took education courses. I ran a nursery school, and then a health food store and restaurant. I left all that and was going to go back to teaching K–3, but the drawback was the low pay and that you were indoors all the time. I had gotten addicted to the outdoors.

So, I evolved into someone who drove a pickup truck to work at eight A.M. every day and was really laboring. It was a good feeling. I felt healthier and at ease. Some of that comes from just getting oxygen into your system. And the John Wayne fantasy is part of it—boys play with guns and hammers and all that. After a while I realized that there was more money to be made working for yourself.

When you begin doing carpentry, first your wrist hurts, then your elbow, then the shoulder. You get used to it, the pain gets buried. But it shows up sometime. I work out at Nautilus to balance my body. I do feel stronger and more durable. I walked eighteen miles the other day. That's not bad for a forty-one-year-old.

I have a truck and I love driving it. It rides higher and smoother than a car. There is something macho about it. It's a better feeling out here with it. It is a locals and nonlocals society here, and I fit in with a truck. There is a pride to saying "I'm a carpenter." You get an interesting response.

I went to college and studied marine biology. I started out wanting to be a dentist, but the prospect of spending my working career with my hands in other people's mouths didn't appeal to me. . . . I stuck with biology and marine sciences. I got a degree, a Bachelor of Arts, and decided to see the country. I had been working as a ferryboat captain. That is how I put myself through college. I bought a 1962 Corvair for $1 and packed my camping gear, skis, et cetera, and went to Vermont. Stayed with some friends there who were doing building. I became a cabinetmaker. No one knew what they were doing. I learned a lot by trial and error. I also had a natural propensity for the work— my father's family had a few boat builders in it. And my mother's grandfather was an upholsterer for the King of Sweden.

My father worked outside as a foreman for an overhead line crew for Lilco. He's in excellent physical condition, so I think I really have a genetic tendency toward that. I feel really comfortable with doing what I am doing. I tried working indoors, and felt cooped up and crummy. With what I am doing now, I am in control over my body. I watch what I eat. I am not a strict vegetarian, but I do eat mostly food without chemicals and no prepared foods.

I want to do the best work I can, and I want everyone who works for me to do the same. It is false economy to do anything but that. There must be a mutual feeling of respect between an employer and his or her crew as well as amongst the crew members. I always felt uncomfortable with the crews that hang out and drink beer and play rock music.

Self-sufficiency is important to me. Sometimes I think about what might happen if there is a severe depression. If anyone would be prepared for that, I would be prepared for it.

(CENTER) I came from a farm. There were ten boys in the family and I migrated to New York in 1973. I quit farming and went traveling. I wound up in New York. There is better pay here and I am happy at construction work. The work is easier than the farm. I wish everyone worked; it would be a better place to live. The only way you can make it is to work. On the farm, expenses were limited. Here you have to buy what you want, there I raised what I needed.

(RIGHT) Work is good for you. It keeps you in shape physically and mentally. It's something to think about. My mom is ninety-four and she always worked and she had eleven kids. If I wasn't working I'd go crazy. I enjoy what I am doing.

(LEFT) It's okay. It's work, you have to do something. I enjoy it, working outside. I pretty much saw myself doing this when I was younger. Started doing it, got used to it, enjoyed it, and then just continued. More than likely I'll do it for ten, fifteen more years—then, I don't know.

Working with my dad [at right in photo] is all right. At first I caught more grief than anyone else. He was able to blow off steam that way. I'm more like the boss now, so it is different.

I work hard six days and then do paperwork on the time off. I come home too tired, the wife doesn't like it.

I don't think about getting hurt.

▲ (RIGHT) I've been doing this work for three years, and I worked summers during high school. My grandfather had done ironwork too. When you hear about what your ancestors did, it makes you feel proud and you want to do it too. It is a family tradition. My father is the boss of this crew and my stepbrother works here too. It is fun to work with family, it makes me want to work steady all the time. We live on the St. Regis Reservation, on the America-Canada border. There are about five thousand Senecas there, and of those, fifteen hundred are steelworkers. We keep an apartment in New Jersey for midweek working; it is too far to drive to the reservation.

▲   I've been doing this—carpentry and demolition work—for about one and a half years, whatever falls my way. I like it and want to get better at the carpentry work. I was going to go to school but I missed registration. They make you go for four years before you can make $21.90 an hour. If I learn by doing and then join the union, I would get full scale with school to my credit.

      Some guys, you look at them, they make $400 a week, everything is going for them, they don't do anything with their lives.

I like working. I like being out on the street and meeting people. Before this I was working in a canning factory.

▲ I like anything I can do with my hands. I didn't like working with wood. I like soldering and outside work—the pipe work. It keeps me interested; it's not repetitious. I like pipe work.

I think work is great. I always see the job progressing. I see the layout first, then little by little I get an idea of where you have to run your water, et cetera. Then you start. You then have a real understanding of what it is about. I really do like it.

I like what I am doing. I enjoy working with my hands. It's interesting work. Getting electricity from the pole to the appliances or into the house—that is a challenge. It is a big responsibility. If you mess up, that's real trouble for people. Gotta know what you are doing, and that's why I'm learning it all now. I go to school three days a week for this.

WARNING

(RIGHT) When you get a compliment on what you are doing, you feel great. I've been doing this for three years. I went to college for one semester and it didn't feel right. It wasn't what I wanted. I feel better now. I felt like I was pressured into doing college and that this working is all my choice. I did it on my own.

The work is good for you physically. You feel like you're putting in a full day's work, not like pencil pushers. Lifting ladders and setting up scaffolding is very hard work, you feel it. But it is not a way to meet girls. You're in areas that are quiet, not like in New York City. You can make a decent living at this work and most girls are surprised at that. You can do especially well if you go into your own business.

(LEFT) We do home improvements, mostly exteriors. I don't mind it, it is something to do. I would go nuts if I did not work. I just couldn't stay home like my wife. Anyway, I have two little kids, two and four years old, and they scream a lot so I have to get out.

I still haven't figured out what I will do with the rest of my life. I am still searching for my niche. I like working with my hands, making the old look like new. There is a real satisfaction when the job is done. It's rough in the winter—I have to wear three pairs of cotton gloves. I look like a poor person; the tips wear off the gloves from the rough work. During the winter it takes a lot out of you. We are on the job from eight-thirty to five. We don't get to know the people too much whose houses we do. An ice cold beer sure feels good at the end of the day—we've earned it as the ad says. I would like to have it a little easier, to have a decent income by doing a little less.

No, this is not what I saw myself doing for the rest of my life. I was going to stay in the Navy—that is where I learned how to do this work. But it is outside work, it's all right. It is pretty repetitive but the wages and benefits are good. Once you start you just tend to stay in it. Don't know why. Right now it's about habit.

I was in Houston in business for myself and I failed during the recession. If I was doing this work in the mountains or climbing poles, it might be more exciting or more dangerous, like it used to be. Now it's more fiber optics. We do underground work mostly. When you get older the romance fades from just about everything. Some days it is a blessed bore, waiting for another problem to happen. Ad infinitum, it seems. This is the first three of six holes, and with darkness descending soon we have to cover up what we have. We don't seem to be making any progress here—that is the worst of it.

This is my third year with this company. It is beautiful to be out here ▶
in the sunlight. I like that, and there are beautiful people in this work.

I love it, laying the pipe and tamping the cement. It feels good to work and to be outside.

▲   I just think about what I am doing when I am working. I keep concentrating and don't worry about any of the dangers. If you start thinking about danger, it might happen. This is good physical exercise, better than weight lifting.

I've been in this town for twenty-one years. The boss and I went to high school together. We do demolition. I take pride in the kind of work I do. I love working—I enjoy what I do.

◄   I've worked all of my life and I love it. The accomplishment and the finishing of a renovation is what I love. It is not about tearing apart. It is about when it starts to go together. There is an elation in finishing the product. I get paid very well for doing this.

What has changed on the jobs is that you always saw waste. Now you see much more. Every change that is done is an extra. When you move the sprinkler system, everything has to be moved and that's all extras then. When I was a kid thirty years ago, I got pleasure from ripping it all apart. As I got older I started to appreciate the finished product.

▼ It is all right. The money's good. It is not that good to work outside in all types of weather. I didn't think about what I'd be doing. Sometimes this is not safe, but I am not afraid.

▲   We do brickwork, twenty-five years at it. Thirty years ago I came from Italy. It's beautiful here. I keep working and I feel I have the good life. The more I work, the better I feel. There have been lots of changes—some years have been tough that I remember. But mostly it has been good.

◄   The pay is good, the work is hard. I work from eight A.M. to four P.M. My fellow workers are good. I wear a mask for the dust. There are no chemicals and no rashes on this job.

I am saving money. I got a nice girl, I'm going to buy me a car. I'm supporting my son and also living good—not fancy, just like an average guy.

Working is okay. It is better working in the streets than in the field. I'm a pipe layer for the last six years. I drove a truck for a while. You work harder at construction, but in a truck there is no boss. Here—on the job—there are too many bosses, too many inspectors. It's like being henpecked.

I'm married and have two children, six and four years old. Lots of women pass by and wave and holler at you. They like to disturb you. You could say what you want back to them.

After work, we do drink beer, just like we're pictured doing. We're blue-collar workers—we work hard and drink beer. We work daylight to dark and then like to drink beer. It's eight hours of a workout and you get paid for it. I feel tired but rewarded at the end of the day.

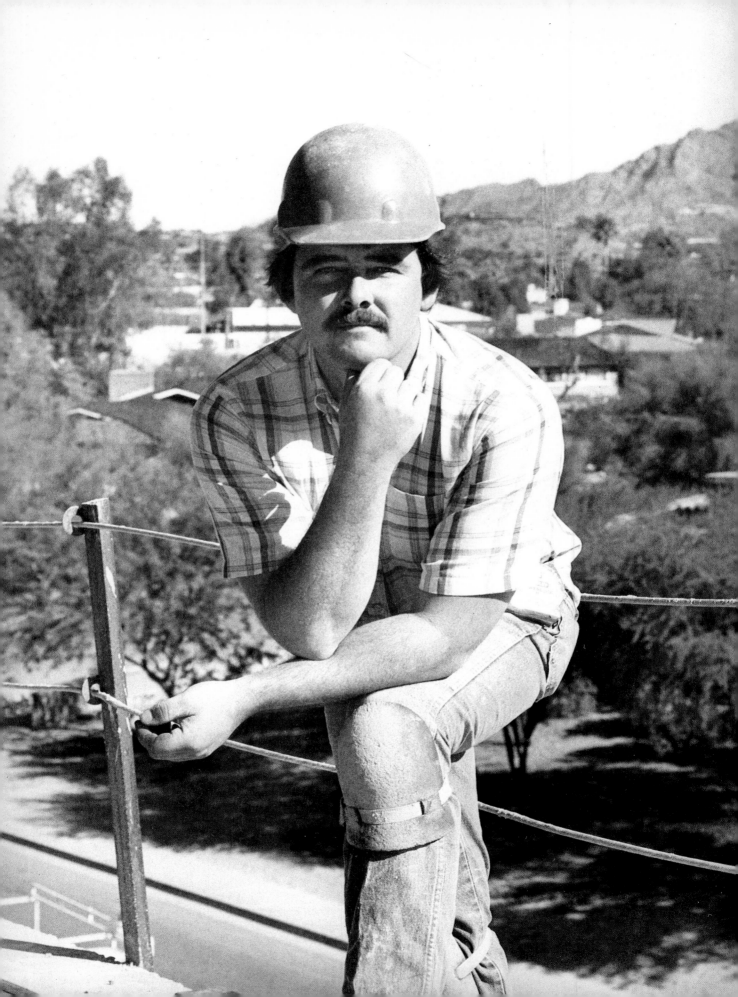

My father was a glazier. I took in his footsteps. When I was young his job looked exciting to me (he did what I do now) and he made good money. I used to make good money here, when I was union. But the shops went non union because of all the building. There was competition from the smaller firms so we all went non union. We do the same thing for less money. It is downhill in Arizona for the trades.

Women are something to take your mind off work—like a small vacation. It takes your mind away from the construction job.

I feel trapped, I have nowhere to go. Lots of times I'd rather be doing something else. But I don't know what that something else is. But I imagine everyone must feel like that at times—even doctors, any trade.

◄   I feel great, outdoors in the fresh air. I have worked all over the western half of
the United States for the last sixteen years. I did nuclear powerhouses. It was safe because
ours was the first part. I got tired of traveling, the kids are older. They and we like to
stay put now.

       As I get older, I think I'd like to try something else—a second career.

(RIGHT) My dad has a nursery, and that is where I started working. I went to college for two years, a community college, and couldn't be behind a desk. School didn't help me. I've worked since I was six and I love it. I'm outdoors, get in shape. It's creative work—taking a bunch of shrubs or brick and making it look aesthetically pleasing. This is the fifth year I've been in my own business. I do retaining walls, brickwork, landscaping. Someone has to do it.

I was lucky to have a good start. My dad is a great craftsman. He taught me to do things right or don't do them at all. Because of the way he taught me, I've gotten a lot of satisfaction from my work. It's not only to make the customer happy, it's good to look at something nice that you've made. When I was young, I wanted to be a musician. I spent a lot of time playing guitar. Then the band fell apart. I was upset for a long time. Now I look back, and I get together with my musician friends—it's a rough life with drinking and drugs. It took me a long time to get over the disappointment of not making it with the music—and seeing how bad it is with some of them.

I always did a lot of carpentry. I studied karate for seven years, and now I am most interested in flying. I'd like to integrate my hobbies with my work. If I have to travel, I'd like to be able to fly there. Maybe I'd retire or teach karate. During the day, most of the time, I try to make it like a good meditation—becoming immersed in the work and forgetting about your normal everyday thoughts. Also, if I have something to look forward to like flying after work, then I feel great.

People who live out here, east end of Long Island, want quality work. If I lived in the woods, I couldn't be doing first-class work. There wouldn't be the customers for it. This area is beautiful that way.

Definitely, this work helps your body—moving all the time. My dad is fifty-seven. He's in great shape—works hard, sleeps well. Eating right gives me more stamina. I try to eat food close to the way nature intends it to be—fish, no meat, and lots of whole grains. When I was young, I wasn't pleased to be tall and skinny—always looked young. Now it's all muscle. I look better than the guys from high school. I do karate on my own, so I don't need a regular workout.

The image of the construction worker is coarse and inconsiderate, but not the people I'm working with. Lots of men think that way, but they don't voice it (like in an office). But if you're on a job with all men, it comes out. I look and appreciate a nice-looking woman and man. I don't act differently when I am around my wife. The older generation used to say not to talk that way around women, but on the job they would say anything. You should be able to say what you want in front of everyone, or not say it at all.

Working with wood is satisfying. Wood has spirit. It once was alive. There is something nice about moving a real sharp plane on a piece of wood and making a nice glossy finish.

▲   For fifteen years, I've been doing this road work. It's fun trenching. We dig Arizona. I make money and get involved in physical work. In my previous work [driving a truck] there used to be a lot of sitting around.

I'm the foreman and I have no problems with the guys. Black, Mexican, and white—we hire everyone. It works better to be mixed races. It seems as if they work together better if they are not all of one kind.

I love this kind of work.

I've been working since the fifth grade—landscaping, into construction, a jack-of-all-trades, manager of a gas station, manager of two departments in a store. I couldn't stay there because I felt closed in. I always wind up coming back to construction. It's something different all the time.

We have a good crew, and that is important. We have disagreements here and there, but we know what's got to be done. Everyone is willing to help out if you are in a bind.

The work is a good workout. Lifting rubber roofing, eight hundred to a thousand pounds, and then going up and down the ladder keeps me in physically good shape. I have diabetes and some days it is hard if the work goes on a long time. I keep food in the truck, just in case.

Eventually I may homestead in Vermont. I like the country attitude, with people helping people out. On my day off, I have no idea what to do!

▲   I enjoy the guys I work with more than the work itself. I get a good tan and good workout all summer. Sometimes the work is monstrous. An example would be grading a lawn by yourself all day. It's ridiculous.

I go back to school soon. I'm a senior. I like working for a friend. If I come to work late or miss a day because of drinking, I feel bad that I have to put him in that position. We each give a little. He's more understanding, and I've calmed down a bit. I have no real idea about what to do in the future—maybe a cop, or real estate, or sports management. I'm taking physical education at school.

▲   It's just a job. It's hot, the welding. It is a dying trade—they are flooding the market with welders. It is low pay to start with and the starters are inexperienced—they can't do what I can do. I've been doing this since I was seventeen years old.

▲   When I'm on the street, there are lots of women. They honk their horns and
yell at you.   It's fun.

▲   I'm a foreman. It's okay, it's good for me. I'm a foreman just six months now. It's better pay, keeps me more involved.

(RIGHT) I don't know my career plans. I'm attending school, so I work construction on breaks and summers. It's a pleasant atmosphere outdoors. The crew is young. There are eight to ten of us, and we get along real well. It's a good way to live. It's hard, but it's not that you are asked to go over your limits. It's decent working conditions. Some days you have to hustle, and some days it's skating.

I love what I do. There are not many jobs that you can stand back and look at what you do. Hell of a lot of people won't do it [climb the girders], but we will and we are damn good. Wherever we work, nobody has ever been before. We're like the cowboys of the sky, like the pioneers of the last frontier.

I worked indoors for the telephone company. I worked on the directory but I couldn't stand being cooped up. I had a friend in the construction business, so I took a test. It had math, spatial abilities, mechanical ability, and I got into the apprentice unit. Now I go to school two nights a week. It is a three-year program, but most of what I learn is really on the job.